# Our Earth

### Carlie Todoro

Rosen **REAL** READERS

Rosen Classroom Books & Materials
New York

We live on Earth.

Earth has many kinds of places.

Earth has tall mountains.

Earth has grassy hills.

Earth has forests with many trees.

Earth has islands.

Earth has lakes you can swim in.

Earth has oceans and beaches.

Earth has deserts. This desert has a lot of sand!

Earth is our home.

# Words to Know

desert

forest

islands

lake

mountains

ocean